Tutankhamen's Gift

Written and Illustrated by
Robert Sabuda

ATHENEUM   1994   NEW YORK

Maxwell Macmillan Canada
Toronto
Maxwell Macmillan International
New York   Oxford   Singapore   Sydney

Atheneum
Macmillan Publishing Company
866 Third Avenue
New York, NY 10022

Maxwell Macmillan Canada, Inc.
1200 Eglinton Avenue East
Suite 200
Don Mills, Ontario M3C 3N1

Macmillan Publishing Company is part of the
Maxwell Communication Group of Companies.

First edition
Printed in Hong Kong by South China
Printing Company (1988) Ltd.
10 9 8 7 6 5 4 3 2 1
The text is set in 14-point Isbell.
Each picture was made from a single
cut piece of black paper adhered to
painted handmade Egyptian papyrus.

ISBN 0-689-31818-9
Library of Congress Catalog Card Number: 93-5401

For my brother Bruce and sister-in-law, Dina
Congratulations!

(and for Tammy and Reba, of course!)

Long ago by the sands of the Nile River a great
Egyptian queen gave birth to her last son. The child
was small and frail and sometimes all but forgotten
among all the children of the royal household. Portraits
of the family, by custom, could only include the
daughters. But even if the sons had been shown,
the littlest boy, Tutankhamen, might still
have been left out.

Yet, no matter how small, all the sons of the mighty Pharaoh Amenhotep III, ruler of Egypt, needed to be educated. So each morning, practically unnoticed, the little child Tutankhamen traveled to the house of the *menoi*, or tutors. There, with the other princes, who were children of royal visitors from distant lands, he quietly practiced his writing. When asked to speak aloud the words of foreign languages they were learning, his voice was the softest.

In the afternoon the princes wrestled, swam,
and practiced archery. But since he was so small,
Tutankhamen did not excel at sports.
   "Do not worry," said his *menoi*, "you are a bright
child and someday your gift for the gods will be revealed."
So Tutankhamen played by himself, making
sparks with his spark maker or racing
with the royal dogs.

On his way home to the palace at the end of each day, Tutankhamen always stopped to watch his father's craftsmen. The pharaoh believed it important to build things to glorify the many gods he and the Egyptians worshiped. It seemed there was always a new temple being raised. Tutankhamen would watch, ignored by all, while workmen prepared huge blocks of sandstone to erect a wall of such a temple.

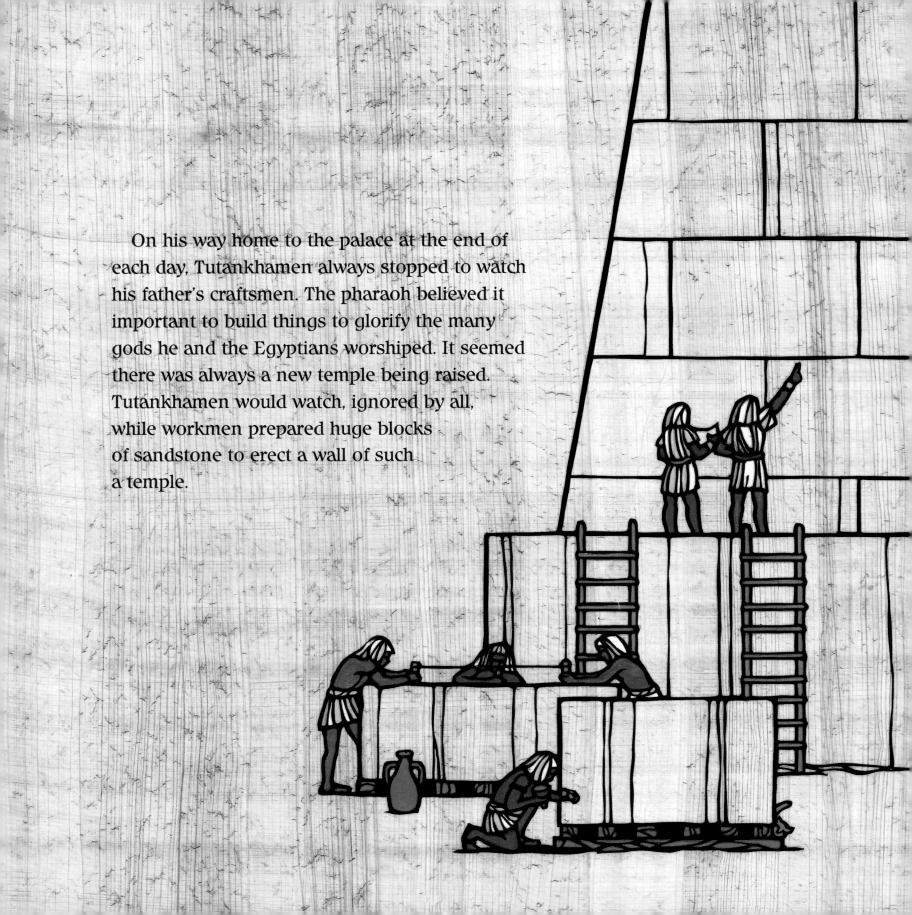

He gazed with admiration
as craftsmen used hammers and
chisels to sculpture images of the
gods or scenes of great battles
on those walls. Later,
painters would come
and dip their papyrus
brushes into pots of
brightly colored inks to
embellish the scenes.

After visiting a new temple Tutankhamen often sneaked into the sculptors' studio to watch the artists create beautiful statues to place inside the temple. Some of the statues were made of solid gold, and they dazzled in the brilliant Egyptian sun. All this to please the gods and keep them happy! Someday, thought Tutankhamen, I too shall do something great to honor the gods. But catching his reflection in a nearby pool, he saw just a small boy slowly making his way home.

Then one day the great pharaoh,
his body old and tired, died.

Sorrow enveloped the land. Women threw
dust in their hair and wept. The men left
their faces unshaven, and no celebrations
of any kind took place. Ruled by
Amenhotep III, Egypt had enjoyed one
of the most prosperous times in its
history. Like all Egyptians, Tutankhamen
sadly wondered if such times could
continue without his great father.

The pharaoh's eldest son, Amenhotep IV,
assumed his father's power. The people
were hopeful, but Amenhotep IV was
not like his father at all. He proclaimed
that all of Egypt should worship only one god,
the god of the sun. He commanded that all temples
built to honor other gods be destroyed.

Soon after, when Tutankhamen walked home from the house of the *menoi* he passed the same workmen and craftsmen as before. But instead of using their great hammers and chisels to create things of grace and beauty, they used them to destroy. Images of the gods were scraped off the walls of many temples, and the blocks of the temples were pulled down. The golden statues were put in ovens and melted. Even monuments raised to honor Tutankhamen's father were not spared.

In a short time the abandoned rubble of the temples was overgrown with weeds and covered with windblown sand. Tutankhamen still visited the temples, but wild dogs roamed through them, and eventually it was no longer safe. The people of Egypt whispered that the gods were angry and had forsaken them, and indeed it seemed true. "The gods have left us because they have no holy places in which to dwell," the people cried. Tutankhamen felt lost and alone without the comfort of the mighty temples his father had built.

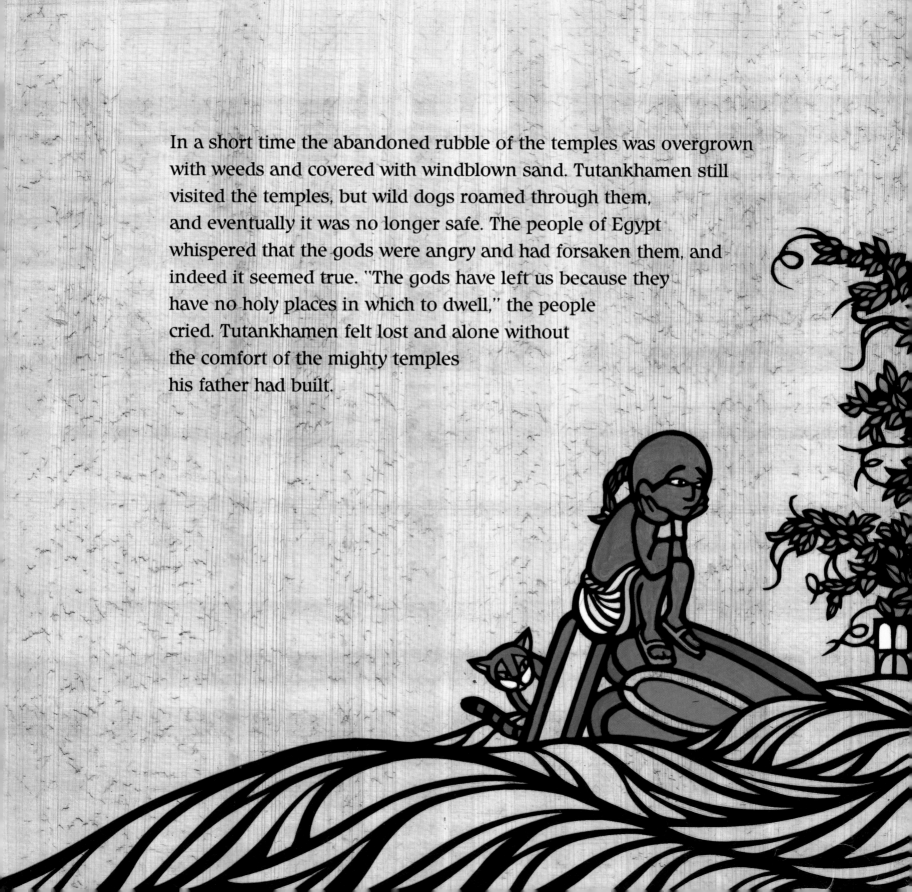

Suddenly Tutankhamen's brother
died. The young pharaoh's death
was mysterious, but the people did
not mourn for him. They mourned
for themselves and their future.
"We need a new leader to guide
us," they said. "Who will bring us
back to the gods? Egypt
must have a pharaoh!"
But who in the royal family
could answer such a call?
All eyes turned to Tutankhamen,
many as if seeing the child for
the first time. He was only ten
years old, so small, so meek.
Could this child really be the last
heir to the throne of Egypt?
Could a boy be pharaoh?

Then Tutankhamen heard a
soft voice that came as if blown
across the desert sands. It was a
voice that grew from the hope
and dreams of his great land,
a voice that he alone could
hear. "Evil is seen best through
the eyes of a child. Only the
young can banish it and cause
the truth to flower once more."

Tutankhamen, last son of the great pharaoh Amenhotep III, turned to his people and proclaimed, "I, Tutankhamen, am pharaoh, ruler of Egypt. I shall rebuild the temples and fill them with monuments to the gods so the people will again have faith. I shall lead the people of Egypt through their suffering and tears so they believe in themselves once more. This will be my promise to you and my gift to the gods."

The people knelt before the boy and vowed with their lives to follow him.

And the boy Tutankhamen restored
the temples of the land and ruled over
the people, it was said, with kindness
and a true heart until the end of
his days.

NOTES ON THE TEXT

Historical facts from such ancient civilizations as Egypt's are often difficult to determine and are much debated by scholars.

Tutankhamen came to the throne at about age nine or ten, during the mid-1300s B.C. His reign lasted only nine years, until he died at age nineteen or twenty. For a long time his death had been a mystery, but recent evidence shows he suffered a blow to the head, possibly during a hunting accident. Perhaps he was murdered. Because he had no living children (two babies died before birth), his death ended the royal line of succession.

Tutankhamen's older brother also died mysteriously. And although many consider Egyptian art to have reached its most creative height during his reign, the people despised him. They called him "scoundrel," and after his death all images of him were removed from the temples and monuments he had built. Even his palace was completely abandoned and left to ruin in the desert.

Much to the relief of everyone, when Tutankhamen came to the throne he reinstated all the old gods. And even though his reign was short, he built more monuments and temples during that time than any other pharaoh.

In A.D. 1922 the British archaeologist Howard Carter discovered Tutankhamen's small burial chamber in the Valley of the Kings, where many pharaohs were laid to rest. The treasures found inside (including Tutankhamen's spark maker) are among the greatest archaeological finds of the century. His was the first tomb of the ancient Egyptian kings that was almost completely intact at the time it was discovered.

—R. S.